Samantha
on a Roll

LINDA ASHMAN • Pictures by CHRISTINE DAVENIER

MARGARET FERGUSON BOOKS

Farrar Straus Giroux
New York

To the McCrimmon family,
and especially Skye
— *L.A.*

Distributed in Canada by D&M Publishers, Inc.
Color separations by KHL Chroma Graphics
Printed in June 2011 in China by South China Printing Co. Ltd.,
Dongguan City, Guangdong Province
Designed by Roberta Pressel
First edition, 2011
1   3   5   7   9   10   8   6   4   2

mackids.com

Library of Congress Cataloging-in-Publication Data
Ashman, Linda.
    Samantha on a roll / Linda Ashman ; pictures by Christine Davenier.—
1st ed.
        p.   cm.
    Summary: Warned not to try out her new skates, Sammy straps them on
anyway, resulting in a wild ride through town.
    ISBN: 978-0-374-36399-4 (alk. paper)
    [1. Stories in rhyme.   2. Roller skating—Fiction.   3. Behavior—Fiction.]
I. Title.

PZ8.3.A775Sam 2011
[E]—dc22

                                                                              2009037308

No, Samantha.
Not today.
Please, go put those skates away.
You're still too small.
You don't know how!
I can't help you—not right now."

But Samantha cannot wait.
Straps herself into a skate.
Straps herself into the other.
Tries them on despite her mother.

Sammy stands and rolls a bit.
Says, "I KNEW these skates would fit!
I'll just try them in the hall.
Mama wouldn't care at all."

(Mama, talking to Aunt Joan,
WOULD have cared, if she had known.)

Sammy skates from here to there—   The bookcase to the rocking chair,

Through the kitchen, through the den,   Down the hall and back again.

Sammy likes the way they glide.
Longs to try those skates outside.
"Why not?" she says. "I'm doing fine.
I'm sure that Mama wouldn't mind."

(Mama, busy bathing Spot,
WOULD have minded quite a lot.)

One more loop across the floor,
Then Samantha's out the door.
Down the sidewalk,
Toward the street,
Roller skates strapped on her feet.

Rising upward—
What a thrill!—
To the top of Hawthorn Hill.

Oh, the view! The park, the pond,
The houses, streets, and farms beyond,
The baseball fields and swimming pools,
The trees and gardens, shops and schools.
A scene of such tremendous scope . . .

She doesn't note the long, STEEP slope.

Slow at first, she glides downhill.
Quickly then,
And quicker still,
Till the scenery's blurring past—
Sammy's going VERY fast!

(Meanwhile Mama, changing John,
Doesn't realize Sammy's gone.)

Will is chasing butterflies.
Sammy takes him by surprise.
Flying by him like a jet,
Carries off his insect net.

Matt and Molly, playing ball,
Miss the frantic warning call.
Sammy stumbles, bumping Matt—
Winds up with his baseball bat.

Toward the park now, swerving right,
Snags the string of Katie's kite.
Katie hollers, "Come back NOW!"
Sammy cries, "I don't know how!"

Now there's music. Someone's singing.
Outdoor wedding. Bells are ringing.
Whiz! Whoosh! Zip! Zoom!
Straight ahead—
The bride and groom!

Sammy tries to move aside.
It's too late—they all collide.
The bride is down. The groom is pale.
Sammy wears the bridal veil.

Now she's heading into town.
Tries to brake, but can't slow down.
Oh, what's this? The town parade!
She veers around the fire brigade,
Slaloms through the marching band,
Overturns the ice cream stand.

Just beyond: a skateboard camp.
Sammy's racing toward the ramp.
"Hey, look out!" a camper cries.
Sammy, frightened, shuts her eyes.

Can't stop herself.
Can't turn around.
She hits the ramp.
She's off the ground.
Sammy's soaring out of sight—
Lifted up by Katie's kite!

Sammy drifts above the town.
Lets the net and bat fall down.

Hears the bride's unhappy wail.
Drops the lacy bridal veil.

Higher then,
And higher still,
To the top of Hawthorn Hill—
Carried by the summer breeze,
Sails into a clump of trees.

(Mama, making Sammy's snack,
Calls her name . . . hears nothing back.)

Sammy looks between her feet.
"Hey!" she hollers. "It's my street!"

Scrambles down and wipes her face.
Dashes home at lightning pace.
Up the sidewalk,
In the door,
Collapses on the playroom floor.

Removes a skate.
Removes the other.
Just in time—
Here comes her mother!

Sammy, flustered, grabs a book.
Dives into the reading nook.

Mama says, "Well, there you are!
I knew you wouldn't go too far.
What a perfect child you've been—
Want to give those skates a spin?"

Sammy sighs. "Oh, that's okay.
I'll try them on another day."